Oh, Bother!
NO ONE'S LISTENING!

Story by Betty Birney
Illustrated by Darrell Baker

A GOLDEN BOOK • NEW YORK
Western Publishing Company, Inc., Racine, Wisconsin 53404

"Do you know what today is?" Piglet asked Winnie the Pooh one especially bright and cheery morning.

Pooh was trying to think of an answer when a loud bouncing sound interrupted him.

"Isn't it a beautiful, bouncy, happy day?" shouted Tigger as he bounced all around Pooh and Piglet.

"Yes, it is," agreed Piglet. "In fact it's the first day of spring!"

"Let's have a First-Day-of-Spring Party," said Pooh, "with lots of honey!"

"And lots of bouncy games!" yelled Tigger.

"And we'll invite Christopher Robin," added Piglet.

"What a splendid idea," said Rabbit when his friends
told him about the party. "But we need a plan."

Everyone gathered in Rabbit's garden to prepare for the
First-Day-of-Spring Party.

"The party will begin at three o'clock at the six pine
trees," Rabbit said.

Pooh and the others shouted for joy.

"Quiet, everyone!" shouted Rabbit. "I will read from my list so that each of you will know what to bring to the party."

Rabbit cleared his throat and spoke up even louder. "Piglet, you bring haycorn pie and lemonade. Tigger, you bring the decorations," instructed Rabbit.

But Tigger was too busy bouncing up and down to listen to Rabbit. And Piglet was too busy trying to stay out of Tigger's way to listen.

1. PIGLET
HAYCO
PI

2. TIGGER
CORATION

Rabbit continued reading from the list. "Owl, you can
bring a kite for us to fly."

But Owl was too busy telling a story about another party
to listen.

"Eeyore," continued Rabbit, "you can bring balloons to the party." But Eeyore was too busy looking at the clouds to listen.

"It will probably rain," said Eeyore as he gazed upward. "It always does when I want to go to a party."

"*I* will bring the tablecloth," Rabbit announced. "And, Pooh, you bring Christopher Robin."

"Brzzlsm?" said Pooh. But he was too busy looking for honey in his honey pot to hear what Rabbit said.

"Are there any questions?" Rabbit asked.

But Tigger, Piglet, and Pooh were too busy dancing about to ask questions.

"A party! A party! We're having a party!" they sang.

Then everyone left to get ready for the party. Owl flew away to his house while Tigger bounced off through the wood. Pooh and Piglet hurried to their houses, too.

But when Piglet got home, he couldn't remember what it was that Rabbit told him to bring.

"A clock? A sock?" Piglet wondered. Suddenly, he looked down at his table. "A tablecloth! That's what I'm supposed to bring to the party."

Eeyore had the same problem trying to remember what he was supposed to bring.

"It couldn't be thistles because I'm the only one who eats them," thought Eeyore. "What could it be? A piece of rope? A bar of soap?"

Nothing seemed quite right until Eeyore noticed his tablecloth. "That must be what I'm supposed to bring—a tablecloth."

Across the Hundred-Acre Wood, Pooh paced back and forth, trying to remember what it was that Rabbit had told him to bring to the party.

"Oh, bother! I wish I had been listening to Rabbit instead of eating honey," he moaned.

"Think, think, think," moaned Pooh. "What do you need for a party—besides honey?"

Just then, Pooh looked down at his table. "That's it! You need a tablecloth for a party! That's definitely what I'm supposed to bring!"

On the way to the six pine trees, Pooh met Piglet. Pooh was carrying his yellow-and-white-checked tablecloth. Piglet was carrying his pink-and-white-checked tablecloth.

"That's strange," said Pooh. "I wonder why Rabbit asked us both to bring tablecloths."

"Perhaps it's a very large party," Piglet replied.

When they arrived at the six pine trees, Pooh and his friends realized that something was wrong. Spread on the ground were FOUR tablecloths, all in different colors.

But there was no food, no decorations, and no Christopher Robin!

"If you think the party's bad now, wait until it starts to rain," said Eeyore, looking up.

Just then, Christopher Robin was walking near the six pine trees. He was surprised to see his friends sitting on the ground with four tablecloths spread before them. Pooh and Piglet each held a tablecloth, too.

"That looks like a very strange game," Christopher Robin thought.

When Pooh saw Christopher Robin, he tried to explain how he and his friends all forgot what to bring to the party."

"Ah-ha," said Christopher Robin. "I think I understand the problem. Nobody was listening to Rabbit. And if no one listens, everyone gets confused."

Christopher Robin turned to Rabbit. "Read from your list again, Rabbit. And this time, everybody will listen."

Once again everyone headed home except Christopher Robin and Winnie the Pooh.

"I wish you would leave," said Pooh. "Then I could get you and bring you back to the party."

"Silly old bear," said Christopher Robin.

But he did leave so that Pooh could get him and bring him back to the party.

This time, because they had listened, each friend brought exactly the right thing.

The party was absolutely perfect...for a while.

Then the little gray gloomy cloud which Eeyore had
been watching suddenly became a little gray gloomy cloud
filled with rain!

"It always happens like this," said Eeyore. "We might as
well go home."

"I have a better idea," said Christopher Robin. "Just
listen."

Pooh and his friends made a tent out of the tablecloths
and the party continued. It was even more fun inside the
colorful tent.

"Tomorrow let's have a Second-Day-of-Spring Party,"
said Pooh.

Eeyore looked gloomy.

"It won't be as much fun," he predicted. "Because with
my luck, tomorrow it won't rain at all!"